FREESTYLE FRENZY

AND OTHER STORIES

STARSCAPE BOOKS BY DAVID LUBAR

Novels

Flip
Hidden Talents
True Talents

Monsterrific Tales

Hyde and Shriek
The Vanishing Vampire
The Unwilling Witch
The Wavering Werewolf
The Gloomy Ghost
The Bully Bug

Nathan Abercrombie, Accidental Zombie Series

My Rotten Life
Dead Guy Spy
Goop Soup
The Big Stink
Enter the Zombie

Story Collections

Attack of the Vampire Weenies
And Other Warped and Creepy Tales

The Battle of the Red Hot Pepper Weenies
And Other Warped and Creepy Tales

Beware the Ninja Weenies
And Other Warped and Creepy Tales

Check Out the Library Weenies
And Other Warped and Creepy Tales

The Curse of the Campfire Weenies
And Other Warped and Creepy Tales

In the Land of the Lawn Weenies
And Other Warped and Creepy Tales

Invasion of the Road Weenies
And Other Warped and Creepy Tales

Strikeout of the Bleacher Weenies
And Other Warped and Creepy Tales

Wipeout of the Wireless Weenies
And Other Warped and Creepy Tales

TEENY WEENIES

FREESTYLE FRENZY

AND OTHER STORIES

DAVID LUBAR

ILLUSTRATED BY BILL MAYER

STARSCAPE

A TOM DOHERTY ASSOCIATES BOOK
NEW YORK

FREESTYLE FRENZY AND OTHER STORIES

Copyright © 2019 by David Lubar

Illustrations copyright © 2019 by Bill Mayer

A Starscape Book
Published by Tom Doherty Associates
175 Fifth Avenue
New York, NY 10010

www.tor-forge.com

Library of Congress Cataloging-in-Publication Data

Names: Lubar, David, author. | Mayer, Bill (Illustrator), illustrator.
Title: Teeny weenies tales : freestyle frenzy and other stories / David Lubar ; illustrated by Bill Mayer.
Description: First edition. | New York : Starscape, 2019. | "A Tom Doherty Associates Book." | Summary: A selection of twelve stories about mermaids, wishes-come-true, and other peculiar things with comic-book style illustrations.
Identifiers: LCCN 2018047176| ISBN 9781250173508 (hardcover : alk. paper) | ISBN 9781250187741 (ebook)
Subjects: LCSH: Paranormal fiction. | Children's stories, American. | CYAC: Supernatural—Fiction. | Short stories.
Classification: LCC PZ7.L96775 Tee 2019 | DDC Fic]—dc23
LC record available at https://lccn.loc.gov/2018047176

Our books may be purchased in bulk for promotional, educational, or business use. Please contact your local bookseller or the Macmillan Corporate and Premium Sales Department at 1-800-221-7945, extension 5442, or by email at MacmillanSpecialMarkets@macmillan.com.

First Edition: April 2019

Printed in the United States of America

0   9   8   7   6   5   4   3   2   1

*For all my gamer friends, whether
they are Mystic, Valor, Instinct,
or none of the above.*

Thank you for being there.

CONTENTS

FREESTYLE FRENZY

FRENZY

AND OTHER STORIES

FREESTYLE FRENZY

Who needs an alarm clock when you have a dog who likes to yank off your covers as soon as the sun rises? Not me. Tugger, my adorable two-year-old Sheltie mix, loves to wake me up early. If yanking my blanket doesn't do the trick, she'll grab my pillow by one corner and pull it out from under my head. If that doesn't work, she'll bark. But it usually works.

That's fine. I had a swim meet that morning.

"Wish I could take you to the meet," I said to Tugger as I was finishing my breakfast.

"Yeah, 'cause the dog paddle is a super-fast stroke," my older brother, Jordan, said. "And a wet dog smells so wonderful."

He can be a total Weenie. And he's the last person who should talk about how things smell. When he comes home after basketball practice, I have to open all the windows in the house. But I didn't feel like trading insults, so I ignored him and scratched Tugger on her back. If I didn't do that, she'd yank at the tablecloth for my attention.

After breakfast, I grabbed my gym bag and headed for the school. It's just three blocks from my house. Tugger followed me to the edge of the lawn, then she flopped down and put her head on her paws. That was as far as she felt like going. But after a yawn and a stretch, she let out a *woof* that I knew meant "Good luck."

"Nervous?" my teammate Angela asked when I got to the locker room.

"Never," I lied.

"We've got this one," she said.

"For sure," I said. I know it's not good to boast or to get overconfident, but Angela and I were one half of a really strong relay team. We'd come close to beating the state record in the 4-by-100 freestyle. This was the last local meet. The winners would go to the regionals, and then to the state championship. It felt great to be part of a strong team.

"Who's that?" I asked when we were getting ready to start the race. I nodded at the lane next to us, where four swimmers I didn't recognize were lined up. They all had long towels wrapped around their waists, covering them all the way to their feet. When the first swimmer on that team hopped up onto the starting block, she didn't let go of her towel.

"No idea," Angela said. "Not that it matters."

It turned out it mattered a lot.

Angela swam first. I was the anchor, going

last. When the whistle blew and the swimmers dived into the water, the girl in the lane next to us finally dropped her towel as she leaped off the block.

That has to slow her down, I thought. Fractions of a second can make a difference. But even though she hit the water behind the others, she quickly made up the lost distance and then started to pull ahead.

"Go, Angela!" I screamed. She was holding on to second place, but was half a body length behind the lead. The next two swimmers on the towel team also shot through the water like fish fleeing a shark. The lead grew greater.

Now it was my turn. We were at least five yards behind when I dived into the pool. The swimmer next to me had already dived in, doing the same strange thing with her towel as her teammates. They all stayed wrapped up in their towels when they weren't in the water.

I tried my best to catch up, but it was impossible. The anchor on the other team was even faster than the first three swimmers.

We were way behind the winners, but ahead

of all the other teams in our heat. Our time would probably be good enough to get us into the finals, but if the team with the towels swam the same way again, our hopes for the regionals would be destroyed.

I looked over at them again. I noticed they 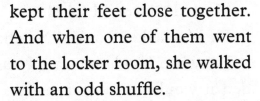 kept their feet close together. And when one of them went to the locker room, she walked with an odd shuffle.

An idea hit me. It was so wild, I pushed it out of my mind right away. But it kept creeping back, like a dog sneaking back to the dinner table after being carried away. So I shared it with Angela.

"No way," she said. "That's totally ridiculous."

"It makes sense," I told her. "I can't think of any other explanation."

"Then keep thinking," Angela said. "Because there has to be."

There wasn't. I got more and more sure my wild idea was the only possible explanation.

We were swimming against mermaids. If that was the case, there was no way we could win.

No. There was one way. It was another wild idea, but it was all I could think to do. I borrowed a phone from a friend in the bleachers, and called my brother.

"I need a favor," I told him.

He laughed and said, "No chance."

But when I told him what I wanted, he decided it would be fun. The best way to get a Weenie to do something is to make him think it's a prank.

I watched the clock. I hoped Jordan would get here in time. He wasn't the fastest kid. He liked to slack off. I guess he'd decided to do just that, and let me down, because by the time the last race started he hadn't shown up.

Once again, the other team pulled into the lead.

The lead widened with the second and third swimmers. It was hopeless. Even if I swam like a speedboat, I'd never catch up.

Right before the fourth leg, as the other swimmer prepared to drop her towel and dive in, I saw someone slip open the side door and peek inside.

It was Jordan. I hoped he wasn't too late. He flashed me a smile, like we were sharing a joke, then put down Tugger. I guess he thought Tugger would run wild, bark at people, cause a commotion, and maybe dive into the pool. He had no idea what I expected to happen.

It didn't matter, as long as it worked.

Tugger looked around, and then dashed toward me. I kept an eye on my teammate, so I wouldn't miss my dive, but I glanced toward Tugger, too.

Don't let me down, I thought.

And she didn't. Just as I'd hoped, Tugger lived up to her name, and her habit. She ran up to the swimmer next to me, clamped down on the end of her towel, and gave a mighty tug.

As the towel pulled free, the swimmer stumbled back off the starting block. Tugger ran to the other side of the pool with the towel. The girl looked at the water and then toward the locker room, as if she had no idea whether to dive in or run away.

That gave me enough time to get a good look at her. It took me a moment to realize what I was seeing.

Her legs and feet were fake!

She was wearing something that slipped over her tail and ended with feet. Her legs and feet could pass for human at a quick glance, or when churning through the water. But right now, as she hopped, stumbled, and slid toward the locker room, I could see my wild idea was true.

She was some sort of mermaid. So were the other three. They all dashed away.

I had a feeling we'd never see them again. At least, not at a swim meet.

That was fine with me.

I wanted to pet Tugger, who'd run back over to me to show off the towel, but I had to do my part in the race. I dived in, swam hard, and locked in a win for our team. We were going to the regionals!

Then, I got out, hugged my teammates, and petted my dog.

"You saved the day," I said to Tugger.

My hand was wet. But she didn't seem to mind at all. She wagged her tail. Then, she grabbed my towel and ran off back to Jordan, who was waiting for her by the door.

"We're bringing her to the regionals, right?" Angela said. "Just in case."

I smiled and nodded. "Good idea." You never knew what you might run into at a swim meet.

GROUNDHOG
DAY

It's a stupid belief," Myron said.

"Nope," Jasper said as he knelt by the mound.

"Yup," Myron said. "And even if it works, why would we need to know?"

"Because." Jasper spat out that single word, as if the answer were obvious. He leaned over, so his head was directly above the hole.

"You're blocking the sun," Myron said.

"So?"

"So how can the groundhog see his shadow if you do that?"

Jasper opened his mouth to argue. He

disagreed with most things Myron said, because he knew he was
way smarter than his friend. But
no words came. Jasper hated to ad-
mit it, but Myron actually had
a point.

He backed away from the
hole far enough so his shadow wasn't over it.
"I was just testing to make sure there could be
a shadow today."

"Was not," Myron said.

"Was too."

"Wasn't."

"Was."

After several more rounds of "was"
and "wasn't," the weather-watching
Weenies switched from exchang-
ing words to swapping shoulder
punches.

Once they'd grown tired of argu-
ing and hurting each other, Jasper
leaned toward the opening again.

"Maybe there's no groundhog,"
Myron said.

"Has to be," Jasper said.

"Why?"

"Because."

"Because why?"

"Because because."

"*Because* isn't an answer."

"Yes, it is."

"Why?"

"Because."

They waited. They argued. They punched. The sun rose higher. "Really, what's the point?" Myron asked as noon approached.

"We'll know if we might get more snow days at school," Jasper said.

"Oh. That's good," Myron said.

"I know," Jasper said.

They waited.

And they waited.

"I think it's empty," Myron finally said. "There's no groundhog."

"You don't know anything." Jasper got up and backed off, keeping his eye on the groundhog's hole so he wouldn't miss

23

anything. As he inched away, he felt around near his feet until he found a stick. "I'll stir it up a bit."

He thrust the stick into the hole and swirled it around like a giant spoon.

"You'll just scare it off," Myron said.

"Will not."

"Will too."

Again, words led to shoulder punches, but Myron quickly dropped his side of the argument because Jasper had a stick.

"I'm going home," Myron said.

"You'll miss everything," Jasper said.

"There's definitely no groundhog in there."

"Has to be," Jasper said.

Myron turned away. Jasper tossed the stick aside and jammed his face against the hole.

"Hey, you stupid groundhog," he shouted, "come out!"

Then he screamed and leaped to his feet. Blood sprayed from his face like it was a lawn sprinkler.

"I guess there is a groundhog," Myron said. "Did he see his shadow?"

Jasper was too busy screaming to answer the question.

But someone else now knew a bit more about the weather.

Down below the blood-splattered earth, the groundhog backed away from beneath the hole and spat something onto the floor of his burrow.

"Got it," he said.

"I knew he'd lean down eventually," his wife said. "We just had to be patient."

"You were right," he said. "I'm glad we waited."

"One nostril or two?" his wife asked.

"Two," he said, batting at the bitten-off nose with one paw.

"So, that means six more weeks of winter?"

"Yup."

"Good to know," she said, giving him a gentle pat on the shoulder.

"Good to know," he agreed, returning the pat. "Let's go back to sleep."

And so they did.

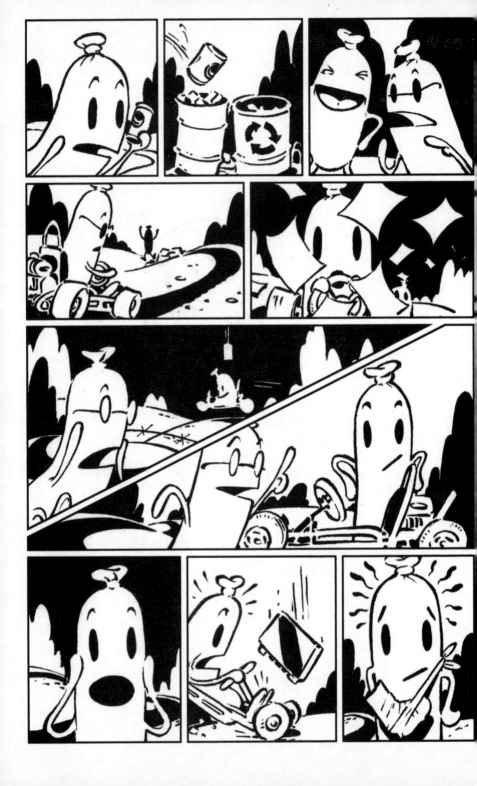

BACK TO EARTH

My friend Rudy and I were on our way home from school when he tossed his empty Orange Zap soda can into the wire garbage basket right outside the front door.

"Wrong container," I said. I pointed toward a blue bucket sitting next to the basket. It had that familiar symbol painted on the side, with three arrows chasing each other around in a circle. "That's the one for recyclables."

Rudy shrugged. "Big deal. One little can doesn't make a difference."

"Yes, it does." I reached into the basket, plucked out the crumpled can, and put it in the recycling bin. "Every little bit makes a difference."

"Yeah. Right." Rudy reached into the bucket, grabbed the can, and tossed it back into the trash, throwing it like he was shooting a three-point basket. "Score!"

I took it out again and put it where it belonged. Rudy grabbed it, spat on it several times, making it pretty much untouchable, and tossed it in the garbage. "Your move."

I decided to let the can go. But I didn't want to drop the topic. "You know what tomorrow is, right?" I asked.

"I sure do. It's the day my dad gets me the new battery for my go-kart. I'm definitely winning that race next week." Rudy turned an imaginary steering wheel and went, "Vrooommmmmmm!"

I knew his go-kart made a sound a lot more like a tiny lawn mower, or a large kitten, than a roaring muscle car, but I let that go, too. "Tomorrow is Earth Day," I said.

"Oh no!" Rudy said, smacking himself in the forehead with his open palm. "I totally forgot to buy it a present. Now it's going to hate me."

I could see there was no point trying to get him to be serious about anything green. This wasn't the first time I'd taken a shot at it. Yesterday, in the cafeteria, he'd done the same thing with an empty glass bottle. And the day before that, in the library, he'd dumped a report in the garbage can, right next to the paper bin. He'd shoved it down past a bunch of tossed-out paper plates that had been left there after a book club pasta party, so there was no way I could rescue the pages and put them where they belonged.

As much as all of this bothered me, I didn't want to annoy Rudy too much, or get too preachy. That wouldn't make him start caring and stop being such a litter-loving Weenie. Besides, even if it was a lot less cool than a dirt bike or an ATV, his go-kart was fun to ride, and he was pretty good about sharing the fun.

When we reached his house, he said, "Hey, come on over tomorrow afternoon. I'll have the new battery in by then. That's the last thing I need to get ready for the race."

"Just be sure to recycle the old one," I said, before I could catch myself.

"Sure. Definitely," Rudy said.

The next morning, I joined a bunch of kids from my church group, picking up trash along the Musconetcong River, near where it empties into the Delaware. That was our Earth Day activity. My folks were going to take me to a concert that evening, at the high school auditorium, in honor of Pete Seeger. He was a folk singer who cared a lot about the environment.

But between the river and the concert, I had time for some go-kart riding. I met Rudy at his place after lunch.

"Ready for some racing?" he asked.

"Sure." Though, with one cart, it wasn't really racing. Still, we could take turns and see who had the fastest time around the course we'd marked out in the vacant lots behind his house.

We'd used wooden stakes to make a course just like the one the races were held on. There were two hairpin turns, an S curve, and a two-seventy loop, so it took a lot of skill to get the best time. Rudy had lost every race last season, so he was really eager to score some wins this year.

He went first. As he was coming out of the last curve into the home stretch, the weirdest thing happened. I missed the beginning of it, because I'd looked away to watch a pair of squirrels chasing each other. But when I looked back, there was a bunch of sheets of paper flying through the air, like Rudy had run into them.

"That was weird," he said when he got off the cart.

I took my turn. But I wasn't going to set a record for the lap, because I stopped along the way to pick up the papers that were scattered on the ground. After I had them all, I folded them and put them under my seat.

"Come on!" Rudy shouted. "Get moving."

I finished the lap. My time would be terrible, but at least the papers wouldn't blow all over the place. As I pulled up next to him, I saw Rudy rubbing his shoulder.

"What's wrong?" I asked after I got off the cart.

He pointed to the ground, where I saw a bottle.

"I think someone threw this at me," he said.

I looked around, There was nobody in sight, not counting the squirrels.

"Maybe it fell out of the sky," I said.

"Very funny." He swung his arm in a circle, flexing his shoulder. "Take another lap. I want to rest this for a minute."

"Sure." That was fine with me, especially since I'd stopped to pick up papers during my first lap.

This time, as I was coming into the last turn, I actually did see what hit Rudy. And it really did fall from the sky. The sunlight flashing off it as it tumbled caught my attention. It bonked Rudy on the head with a *clang* I could hear over the whine of the engine. But at least it wasn't a glass bottle. That would have been really bad.

When I finished my lap and got off the cart, I saw he'd been beaned by a soda can. Good thing it was empty.

"I think we should go inside," I said. I grabbed the papers from the seat and tucked them under my arm. I'd find somewhere to recycle them later.

"No way," Rudy said. "I waited a week for the new battery, and I need to get ready for the next race. I'm riding all afternoon. You can go home if you want. I'm not going anywhere."

Rudy got back on the cart, floored the accelerator, and zoomed off. As the stink of exhaust faded, I sniffed the air. It smelled like someone was cooking spaghetti sauce. But there were no other houses near us beside Rudy's, and I knew his parents didn't like to cook.

I sniffed again, then pulled the papers from under my arm. The one on top had some red stains that looked a lot like sauce. It smelled like sauce, too. I turned the page over. My hand clutched it harder as I realized what I was holding. It was a page from the report Rudy had tossed in the garbage.

I looked down at the bottle. It was Crunch Kola, Rudy's favorite brand.

And the can that just fell was Orange Zap, like the one he'd tossed into the trash yesterday.

Then, something hit me. But not from the sky. The thing that struck me came from my brain. *The Earth was tossing back the things Rudy had thrown out!* If that thought was like a smack to the head, the one that followed was like a dropkick to the gut by a mule with a black belt in karate.

Oh no . . .

The paper.

The bottle.

The can.

The things he hadn't recycled were coming back in the same order they'd been tossed out. I shuddered when I realized what might be falling next.

I looked across the lot, where Rudy had just entered the loop, about halfway around the track.

"Rudy!" I shouted, waving.

"What?" he shouted back.

"What did you do with the old battery?" I yelled.

He shook his head. "I can't hear you."

It didn't matter. I had a feeling I knew the answer. He hadn't recycled the battery. He'd thrown it out.

I looked up above Rudy as he reached the last turn.

"Watch out!" I screamed, pointing at the battery that was dropping from the sky like a ton of lead. Which is sort of what it was, except closer to five pounds, and not all lead.

Thanks to my warning, Rudy hit the brakes, but not soon enough to totally avoid getting clobbered. As he'd said, one little soda can might not make a difference. But one battery surely did.

Rudy was lucky to walk away with nothing worse than a broken arm, three cracked ribs, and a whole new appreciation for the importance of recycling.

I had a feeling Earth Day had finally made a lasting impression on him.

CAN YOU STAND SUCCESS?

"This isn't working," I said to my friend, Katie, as the ten thousandth car drove past us without stopping. About fifteen thousand people had also walked by. Okay, I like to exaggerate, but that's what it felt like.

"You'd think people would want lemonade on a hot day like this," Katie said.

"I sure do," I said as I drank another cup.

"Hey, you're drinking all our profits," Katie said.

"We don't have any profits," I said.

We decided to knock off and go into town. Since we didn't have much money, we headed straight to the old secondhand shop, to see what they had. I found a nice scarf I couldn't afford, and Katie saw a beautiful wallet she couldn't afford. And then, Katie spotted the old book.

"*Wishes,*" she said, reading the title. "*Spells and Potions,*" she added, reading the words below the title.

I looked at the cover. There was a word above *Wishes*. It was all faded except for the last two letters, which were *st*.

"*Best Wishes,*" I said. My parents were always saying that to people who were about to do something important, like get married or start a business. "We could definitely use some of those."

"Maybe there's one that can help us sell lemonade," Katie said.

She flipped the book open and, like magic, we were staring at a spell that promised endless success in business.

"That's worth a try," Katie said.

"I don't know," I said. "Maybe we shouldn't mess around with magic."

Katie ignored me and checked the price written in pencil on the inside cover of the book.

"Hey, I can almost afford this. Can you chip in the rest?"

"I guess." I gave her the money she needed.

After she bought the book, we took it to her house, and gathered up the ingredients for the spell. We had to make a powder, and then sprinkle it on the table where we sold our lemonade. We set the table up again in the morning.

"I hope it works," Katie said.

"Don't get your hopes up," I said.

A car pulled over by the curb. "Oh, thank goodness I spotted you. I need all the lemonade you have," a woman said. "I'm late for a meeting of my book club, and I promised to bring refreshments."

She bought all the lemonade, and the jar we'd made it in.

"Wow," Katie said. "The spell worked."

"We need more lemons," I said.

"And another jar," Katie said. "You go to the store for lemons, I'll get another jar from the basement."

There was a market right down the block. I ran there, bought lemons with some of the money we'd made from the lemonade, and met Katie in her kitchen, where we whipped up another batch.

By the time we got back to our table, there was a line of people waiting for a drink. Before we knew it, we were out of lemonade again, but not out of customers.

"Buy more lemons this time," Katie said. "And cups. We're almost out."

"Find a bigger jar," I said.

We got more supplies.

I was afraid people would leave if they had to wait, but when I got back from the market, the line was even longer, and thirstier.

We made lemonade all day. I kept running back to the market for lemons and sugar. But no matter how fast we worked, the line never got shorter.

"We need to stop," I said to Katie. "I'm exhausted."

"No!" someone in the crowd shouted.

Others shouted, too.

"I've been waiting half an hour!"

"Don't you dare close!"

"I'm back for another cup!"

"This is the best lemonade ever!"

"I brought my whole family this time!"

I realized it would be a bad idea to stop. I didn't want to have to deal with an angry mob.

"Get the book," I said.

"Why?" Katie asked.

"We need to find a spell for business failure," I said.

Katie got the book. When I opened it, I saw the title page, and my heart sank. I'd thought it was a book full of the best wishes. But the title was *Worst Wishes*.

I remembered something my grandmother

45

used to say all the time: "Be careful what you wish for."

I'd never understood what that meant until now.

"Look at this." I showed Katie the page and tapped the title. "We were real Weenies to mess around with spells."

"Worst-wish Weenies," Katie said.

By the end of the day, Katie and I were totally exhausted. We still had customers, but there was nothing we could do about that. The store was out of lemons.

"Sorry, folks," I said before Katie and I went inside. "We're closed."

We ran inside to escape their cries of disappointment.

"I'm glad that's over," Katie said.

"Me, too," I said.

I guess, at that point, neither of us understood just how powerful a spell we'd cast, because the line was still there in the morning. We were greeted with more shouts.

"Look, they're open!"

"It's about time!"

"This will be my tenth cup!"

I raced to a different store for lemons.

"It's going to be a long summer," I said to Katie when I joined her in the kitchen.

"Maybe the spell will wear off," she said.

I sighed, and said the only thing I could. "I wish . . ."

THE SPLINTER

"Yeeoowcchhh!"

All around town, and possibly as far away as neighboring states, folks couldn't help but hear Harlan's shout as the dreadful splinter jabbed its way beneath the skin at the tip of his forefinger.

"OOOWWWWWW! It hurts!" Harlan yelled, jerking his hand back from the porch railing and acting like a complete Weenie.

The splinter—huge as a broomstick and long as a flagpole—jutted from Harlan's finger, throbbing and aching with a pain almost beyond anything he could stand.

"What's all the shouting about?" Harlan's mother asked as she rushed out to the porch.

"I got a splinter," Harlan cried. An instant later, he knew he should never have spoken. As bad as a splinter was—there was something worse in the world. The cure . . .

"Well, stop your hollering," his mother said. "Wait here while I get a needle."

Harlan could feel his stomach shrinking into a shriveled ball. His hair stood on end and his legs turned to cooked strands of spaghetti as he heard the dreadful word.

Needle!

He decided to run to somewhere safe, but his mother was too fast. Before Harlan could even reach the steps, she had returned and grabbed his wrist.

"Here we go," she said, holding up the gleaming needle, sharp as a dagger and cold as a winter night. "I'll have that mean old splinter dug out in no time."

"NOOOO!" Harlan shouted, yanking his hand free. "It will hurt!"

"Nonsense," his mother said, grabbing his wrist again. "Just be still for a moment."

"It hurts!" Harlan screamed. He screamed the same message several more times. Once might have been enough, but Harlan didn't have a lot of control at the moment.

His mother raised the needle and studied Harlan's finger. Harlan braced himself for unbearable pain. His mother looked closer. Harlan waited.

"Where?" she asked.

"What?" Harlan asked.

"Where's the splinter?" she asked.

Harlan looked at his finger. Then, he looked closer. And then, he looked even closer. There was no splinter. He realized that it must have fallen out when he was jerking his hand around. Harlan took a deep breath to calm himself. It was over. No more splinter. No more needle. No more pain.

His mother patted him on the head. "Maybe you imagined it."

"No, really, I had a splinter. Look." Harlan pointed to the tiny hole in the tip of his finger.

"I see," his mother said. "Well, we'd better wash it out with soap and hot water. We don't want to risk an infection." She grabbed Harlan's wrist and led him toward the kitchen sink.

"NOOOO!" Harlan hollered. "It will sting!" And it did.

OPENING DAY #1

"Play ball!"

The umpire's shout rang throughout the stadium.

"Finally!" Jacob said. He'd been waiting months for the most magical day in April to arrive. It was opening day of baseball season, and this was his first time ever in a real stadium.

Until this year, his family had lived far from any stadiums. But they'd moved last winter, and now lived less than two miles from a minor-league ballpark. Ever since then, his parents had promised to take him to a game.

And here he was, sitting in the front row of the upper deck, halfway down the first base line. "These are great seats," he said.

"Just keep your eyes open," his dad said.

As if to prove how good that advice was, the batter swung late and hit the first pitch foul. It shot into the stands, right toward Jacob.

SMACK!

His dad caught it in the glove he'd brought.

"Wow!" Jacob said as his dad plucked the ball from the glove and tossed it to him. "This is the best day *ever!* The only thing that would make it even more amazing was if I could be playing down there."

He pointed toward the infielder who was covering second base. That was his favorite position.

"It could happen someday," his dad said. "If you work hard to achieve your dreams, you can do anything."

"It takes a lot of dedication to become a professional," his mom said. "But I know you can do it if you set your mind to it."

"I can definitely work hard. I'll be down there someday." Jacob turned his attention back to the game. But toward the end of the third inning, his stomach started to distract him by growling. It didn't help that there was a hot dog stand at the top of their section. The smell was calling to Jacob. He loved hot dogs so much, his friends called him "Weenie Boy."

"Can I get a snack?" he asked.

"That's part of the pleasure of the ballpark," his dad said. He handed Jacob some money. "Here. Get us all something."

"Thanks." Jacob slipped out of his seat and squeezed his way past spectators until he reached the steps at the end of the row.

"Be careful," his mom called after him.

"I will," he called back.

Halfway up the steps, and halfway toward a juicy grilled hot dog, Jacob heard the hard *CRACK!* of a solid hit. He spun around just in time to see a line drive sizzle across the infield. It ripped past the pitcher, hit the ground hard, and took a bad hop as the second baseman knelt to scoop it up.

Jacob flinched in sympathy as the ball socked the player in the head. He could almost feel the impact himself as the man crumpled. Other players and the umpire rushed over. They crowded around the fallen second baseman. A trainer came. The whole stadium held its breath, watching and waiting. Finally, the player got to his feet.

He headed for the dugout, helped by his teammates. He was walking shakily, but he managed to wave to the crowd. Everyone cheered for him, no matter which team they were rooting for.

"Ladies and gentlemen, can I have your attention, please," the announcer said. "We need a volunteer to fill in at second base."

Jacob raised his hand and shouted, "I'll do it!" His voice boomed through the air just like the announcer's.

People all around the stadium turned their heads to stare at him. Then, they all applauded.

Jacob made his way to the field, and then trotted to second base. He was happy to discover that the glove the player had dropped wasn't a bad fit for him.

I'm on a real field, he thought. *I'm in a real ballpark, playing in a real game.* He reached down and plucked a couple blades of grass from the ground. He crushed them in his palm and enjoyed the sweet green smell.

"Play ball!" the umpire shouted.

Jacob played. He played hard, and he played great. He made leaping dives and heroic throws. He hit two doubles and a triple. His team, which had been down by three runs when Jacob took his position, was up by three at the end of the eighth inning.

Three more outs and I'm a hero, Jacob

thought as the visitors took their last chance at bat at the top of the ninth inning. He waved to his parents in the stands, and thought about how amazing it would be to become the youngest professional baseball player of all time.

The inning started badly. The other team scored twice, and now had runners on first and second. Jacob wasn't worried. He knew this rally would just give him a chance to look even better when he saved the day for his team.

Jacob caught a sizzling line drive for the first out. It smacked his glove so hard, it almost lifted him off his feet. He dove to snag a grounder from the next batter, then rolled to his feet and snapped a burning throw into the waiting glove of the first baseman for the second out.

The grounder allowed the runners to advance. There were men on second and third now. If the next batter hit a single, that would tie the game. A double would put the other team ahead. The whole stadium was silent as the batter came to the plate. Jacob remembered he was a power hitter who had sent every ball he connected with straight up the center.

I'm ready for this, he thought, as he shifted slightly closer to the base so he could snag the hit when it rocketed across the infield.

He turned toward his parents and flashed a thumbs-up. This would be his greatest moment. He'd make the out, end the game, and have a dazzling start to his career as a professional baseball player.

What a great start it would be! He was batting 1,000. He hadn't made a single error. He'd have the best stats of any player, ever. It was like a dream come true.

CRACK!

Jacob was startled out of his thoughts by the sound of a solid hit. He looked toward the plate just in time to see the ball hissing straight toward him, traveling impossibly fast. He threw up his glove, but he was too late. The ball clobbered him in the forehead.

Jacob went down.

The world turned black and silent before he even hit the ground.

The light trickled back first. The world went from black to gray.

He heard a sound. Someone was calling his name.

He opened his eyes. But he wasn't on the field. And he wasn't on flat ground. He was lying on steps. He rolled over, sat up, and touched his forehead, expecting to find a large bump. But his forehead was fine. He reached around and discovered that the ball had hit him in the back of his head. He winced as his fingers felt the swelling lump.

People were crowded around on both sides, staring at him.

He parents were there. They looked worried.

"I'm okay," he said. "I'm a pro. I can take a hit. That's part of the game. Did we win?"

His dad frowned. "It's just the third inning."

"But I was . . ." Jacob thought about all his heroic efforts in the field and at the plate. Looking back, some of his actions seemed hard to believe.

"You got hit by a foul ball," his mom said.

"No," Jacob said. "Not me. *Him.*" He pointed toward the field. "And it wasn't a foul ball. There aren't any foul balls near second base. It was a line drive."

He dropped his hand as he spotted the second baseman, standing unharmed at his position.

"It was a dream," his mom said.

"Dreams are a good start," his dad said. "Think you can handle a hot dog now?"

"I can handle anything," Jacob said.

He walked up the rest of the steps and got his hot dog. It smelled wonderful. But another smell caught his attention as he got ready to take his first bite—a sweet green smell.

Jacob stared at the hot dog. There wasn't any relish on it. Then, he noticed a green stain on his palm.

He looked at second base again, where he

had plucked a few blades of grass from the infield.

He smelled his hand, and knew his short time on the field had been more than a dream. Now he just had to work hard, so he could make that dream come true for more than a day, and play on a real team all the time.

And he had to remember to always keep his eye on the ball.

THE PET SITTER

Daryl decided he needed to earn some money. There were just too many things he wanted, most of which his parents wouldn't buy for him. He sat down on his couch and tried to think up a good job.

"I could babysit," he said.

His mind offered him the image of a baby with an overfilled diaper.

"Nope, never mind," he said, wrinkling his nose. He realized another reason that would be a bad idea. His parents still got a sitter for him when they went out.

He thought about washing cars, but that seemed like too much work. He also didn't like the idea of sitting in the hot sun selling lemonade. He was much happier sitting at home, watching TV.

"Too bad I can't get paid for that," he said.

As he spoke those words, the perfect idea hit him. "I can be a pet sitter!" He leaped up  from the couch and clapped his hands together. "I can sit somewhere else just as easily as I can sit here. And I'll get paid for it!"

He went to his parents' computer and worked up a flyer. Then he printed it out and put copies on telephone poles all around the neighborhood.

Having done all the hard work, he sat back and waited for someone to call.

Nobody called.

He put up more flyers the next day, in nearby neighborhoods.

Nobody called.

Finally, on the third day, the phone rang.

"Are you available?" a man asked.

"Yes, I am," Daryl said.

He got the address and headed over. The man who answered the door was old and small, barely taller than Daryl.

"Come in," he said. "I have to go out often. I don't like leaving Dulcinea alone."

"I can keep her good company," Daryl said.

"Wonderful," the man said. "But I need to make sure she likes you."

"I'm sure she will," Daryl said. "Animals love me." He'd never had a pet, but he was pretty sure he was telling the truth.

The man led him to a door. "This is her room," he said. "You go ahead. I'll be right there."

"Okay." Daryl stepped inside. The room was empty, except for a large cage. Inside it was the biggest rat Daryl had ever seen, outside of a carnival. It was almost as large as a lap dog.

Daryl fought back a scream. Then he re-minded himself of all the things he was going to buy with the money he earned from pet sitting. If the sight of the pet made his skin crawl, he'd just have to learn to get used to it. He stepped closer. And then, being a sneaky little Weenie, he got an idea how he could make sure the man gave him the job.

"I know what to do. I'm going to pick you up. When that guy sees us together, he'll defi-nitely give me the job." He reached for the latch. "Okay?"

The rat seemed to nod.

Daryl unlatched the door and opened the cage. He reached inside to pick up the rat.

It bit him. Daryl screamed and jumped back, clutching his hand. The rat squealed and leaped from the cage. Then it scurried off, flattened itself in a rodent-like way no lap dog could ever dream of doing, and slipped under a baseboard heater. Daryl could hear shuffling in the walls. And he could feel his chances of a pet-sitting job vanishing.

Oh, no! He thought. *She escaped.*

He was startled by the sound of the door opening.

Daryl tried to babble out an excuse. His words got tangled. "It . . . she . . . I didn't mean . . . accident . . ."

"Oh, dear," the man said as he walked over to the empty cage. "Dulcinea will not like this."

"I'm sorry," Daryl said. "I can help you catch her."

"I can't believe you let her meal escape," the man said. "She gets very cranky when she's hungry. Well, I guess that will be the real test of how much she likes you." He walked over to the side wall to the left of the door and flipped a switch.

Daryl watched as a hatch swung open in the wall. Behind him, he heard the door close. He realized the man had gone out. He also realized something enormous was wriggling through the opening behind the hatch.

It was a snake. It was huge. It was bigger than huge. It was enormous.

It was also enormously hungry.

Dulcinea, it turned out, liked Daryl very much. But not as a friend or a pet sitter.

She liked him as a meal, sitting inside of her.

WATCHING WENDEL

Here it comes, Susan thought, looking at her mother and waiting for those horrible words.

"I have to run to the corner store," her mother said. "I'll be right back, but I need you to watch Wendel while I'm gone."

Susan just nodded. *Calm down,* she told herself as her mother left the house. What could happen in ten minutes? What could happen in six hundred short seconds, even with Wendel the miniature wrecking machine, the two-year-old teeny-Weenie terror tot, the—

Her thoughts were knocked to a halt by a

 crash from the kitchen. "Wendel!" she shouted, running to see the damage. There were pots and pans all over the floor. Wendel had pulled everything out of the bottom cabinets. Susan bent to fix the mess. She knew she didn't have time to put the pots back where they belonged, so she started stacking them on the counter. Just as she got the last one off the floor, there was a thump and a shout from the other side of the house.

She ran from the kitchen, skidded down the hall, and raced into the living room. "Yahoooo!" Wendel shouted. Susan saw he had taken all the cushions off the couch and piled them on the floor. He was leaping from the arm of the couch to the cushions. When he noticed his big sister, he squealed and started crawling under the rug.

"Come back," Susan shouted as she replaced the cushions on the couch. But Wendel ignored her and crawled toward the middle of the rug. Susan stared at the wiggling lump. There was only one way to get to him. She started rolling up the rug. But Wendel didn't stay still. He kept just ahead of her. It was like chasing a bubble in a bathtub. Wendel popped out the end just as Susan rolled up the last of the rug.

"Wendel, stop making me chase you. Please, Wendel," Susan begged. She didn't know how much longer she could keep up with him.

Wendel jumped to his feet and toddled rapidly down the hall. Susan ran to follow, but slipped on the wood floor beneath the rug. By the time she caught her balance, Wendel was out of sight. Frantically, Susan ran from room to room. There was no sign of him. Then she heard squeals coming from upstairs. She raced to her parents' bedroom.

"Wendel!" She looked in disbelief at the mess. Her brother had pulled all the sheets off the bed. She reached for him. He dove under the bed. Susan started to crawl after him. He slithered out the other side and ran from the room. In a flash, he'd skittered down the stairs. Susan was right behind him this time. Wendel made a dive for the kitchen door. Susan grabbed for him and missed. She followed him outside, into the backyard.

After two quick laps around the swing set, it was over. Wendel had more energy, but Susan had longer legs. She clutched him in her hands. He looked up at her and smiled.

"Hug?" he asked.

What could she do? "Hug," she answered, giving her brother a squeeze.

She couldn't be angry with Wendel, but she knew she'd be in big trouble when her mother saw the mess in the house.

I tried my best, she thought.

"Susan, come here."

"Uh oh," she whispered, seeing her mother on the porch. She noticed her mother was holding a bag from the store.

"You're home," Susan said, letting go of Wendel and walking toward the porch. Her brother skittered back into the house.

"I can't believe all this," her mother said.

"I can explain . . ." Susan didn't know what to say.

"I really can't believe this," her mother said. "I was just gone ten minutes. Look at what you did."

"But . . ."

Her mother took something from the bag. "How did you know I was going to put new shelf paper in the kitchen?" She held up a roll of white paper. "I wasn't looking forward to emptying those cabinets. And I certainly didn't want to take up the rug by myself, but I just have to clean the floors. You even stripped the beds so we can wash the sheets. I can't believe you did all this and watched Wendel at the same time." She smiled.

"Actually," Susan said, "Wendel was a big help. He should get most of the credit."

"Now don't be modest. I see that we won't

79

be needing a sitter anymore. It looks like the job is yours from now on."

Susan was about to answer when they were interrupted by a crash from the kitchen.

"I'll take care of it," she said as she ran inside to see what Wendel was up to this time.

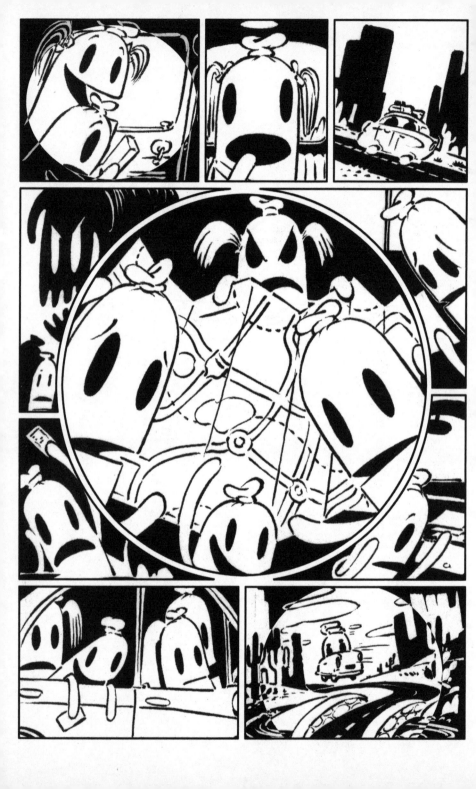

OFF THE MAP

"Herbert, you're missing all the sights," his mom said as they drove down a deserted road, past endless large rocks.

"But I'm slaying a level thirty-eight hydra," Herbert said. He didn't risk looking up from his game. The hydra was a tricky boss.

"You're such a game Weenie," his sister, Olivia, said.

"And proud of it," Herbert said.

"Stop that, you kids," Herbert's father said. "And Herbert, your mother's right. You're missing all the natural wonders we came out here to see. You might as well have stayed home."

"That's what I wanted," Herbert muttered. But he kept his voice quiet enough so nobody heard it except for Olivia.

They drove on, through splendid canyons and towering cliffs. Herbert did his own exploring, in the ancient world of Druidaria. Following directions he'd received at the start of this particular quest mission, he took the severed head of the hydra to the town of Qal'braz.

It was a difficult journey, not only because there were monsters to fight, rivers to cross, and mountains to climb, but also because every five minutes, Olivia would say, "He's playing that game again."

Then, one of his parents would say, "Herbert, put that silly game away."

Herbert would put the game away. But as soon as Olivia got distracted by the scenery, he would slip the game out of his backpack and continue his journey. The fact that the car trip seemed endless meant that, even with the interruptions, Herbert managed to make good progress in the game.

Finally, he reached Qal'braz. Once there, he found his way through winding, narrow streets and alleys, to the home of the alchemist Wizreth the Wise.

Just as Herbert was receiving his reward, and a hint to where he could find his next quest, he felt the car stop.

He looked up, and saw that his father had pulled over to the side of the road.

"What's wrong?" his mother asked.

"Stupid GPS quit working," Herbert's father said. He reached out and tapped his phone, which was clipped to a holder on the dashboard.

"That won't help," Herbert said. He could see quite clearly that the phone was showing the message *No satellite signal*.

 While Herbert wasn't an electronics genius, he was fairly positive that no amount of tapping would bring back the satellite signal.

"Maybe we should just keep driving," his mother said.

"That's all we can do," his father said.

"Are we lost?" Olivia asked.

"No, we're right where we are supposed to be," her father said.

They drove onward.

"We're lost," Herbert's father said half an hour later. "We should have come to a town by now." He pulled over again.

"We can't just stay in the middle of nowhere," Herbert's mother said.

Herbert sighed. It looked like the vacation was about to become even less fun.

"Wait," his mother said. She opened the glove box and felt around. "Here it is! I was pretty sure we had one of these."

Herbert watched as she unfolded a map. The paper was yellow with age, and there were holes worn in some of the creased folds. Both of his parents looked at it. They stared. They turned it different ways. They pointed at various spots and read place-names out loud. They exchanged shrugs.

"I haven't used one of these in ages," his father said.

"I'm not sure I ever did," his mother said.

From the backseat, Herbert noticed that the map looked strangely familiar.

"Let me see," he said, holding his hand out.

His parents frowned at him.

"It's too complicated for you," his father said.

"Please . . . ?" he asked.

They handed him the map. Herbert remembered they'd passed a small lake right after the last time they'd made a turn. He found five lakes on the map. But only one was near a crossroad.

Despite what his parents thought, he really

did look up from his game once in a while to observe the world around him. But what they didn't know was that his game required a lot of map reading. Herbert played so much that he was not just good at reading maps, he was great. And his skill at reading maps in the game worked just as well in the real world.

After checking several more landmarks they'd driven by, he tapped a spot on the map and said, "This is where we are. If you go three and a half miles more, straight ahead, we'll reach a bridge on the left. Turn there, cross the bridge, take the next right, and it will lead us to town."

His parents stared at him like he'd just pulled a hydra out of a hat, or sawed a wyvern in half.

"Do you have a better plan?" he asked.

They drove, reached the bridge, turned left, reached the next turn, where they went right, as directed, and reached town.

As they got out of the car, Olivia pointed at Herbert and said, "He's still playing that stupid game."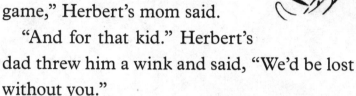

"Thank goodness for that game," Herbert's mom said.

"And for that kid." Herbert's dad threw him a wink and said, "We'd be lost without you."

Herbert didn't look up from his game. He was too busy slaying a level forty-three manticore to take his eyes away from the screen. But the words weren't lost on him. He heard what they'd said. And he smiled.

OPENING DAY #2

"Opening day!" I said, whispering those wonderful words so I wouldn't wake Mom or my brothers. "I thought it would never come."

"But here it is," Dad said. "And here we are, Rachel."

We slipped out to the porch, eased the front door shut, then headed for the car. I loved every moment of our opening-day daddy-daughter fishing trip, from the twinkling stars in the early morning sky to the drive home at the end of the day when, happy and tired, we'd stop for a milk shake at our favorite road-side stand. It was almost as good as my birthday.

"Look at that one," I said, pointing to an especially bright star.

Dad glanced up as he opened the trunk. "I think that's Venus."

After we put our tackle boxes and rods inside, Dad closed the trunk as quietly as we'd closed the front door. We didn't want to wake anybody this early. It was barely past five. The fishing season didn't officially open until eight, but we had a long drive ahead of us, and a hike through the woods to get to the stream.

"Hey, neighbor!"

The shout startled me.

I looked across the street, and saw Mr. Humblebacker stumbling out of his garage, carrying a huge tackle box in one hand and a pair of fishing rods in the other. He was wearing chest waders and a fishing vest. A landing net dangled from his waist, along with a knife in a sheath, a pair of pliers, and a fishing license in a plastic holder.

"Going fishing?" he called.

Dad put his finger to his lips, trying to signal to Mr. Humblebacker that shouting wasn't a good idea when nearly everyone was still asleep. Then he walked across the street.

I stayed where I was, but listened to their conversation. Dad's voice was quiet. Mr. Humblebacker's voice, though no longer a shout, was still pretty loud.

"Taking the little girl fishing?" he asked.

Little? I'm nine. That's pretty grown up.

"Yeah," Dad said. "We're headed up to Foley's Creek."

"Lucky you. I was going to go fishing today." Mr. Humblebacker raised the rods, as if he needed to prove what he said. "I'm quite the avid angler, if I do say so myself. But my car wouldn't start."

Avid angler? More like a fishing Weenie, I thought.

"That's too bad," Dad said

Mr. Humblebacker let out a sigh "I guess

93

I could take a bus to the town park over in Chambersburg, and try my luck at the little pond out there. But that place will be mobbed. Wish I could go to Foley's Creek."

No, Dad! I thought. *Don't fall for it! Don't weaken!*

"Gosh," Dad said. "That would be a long bus ride."

"A very long ride," Mr. Humblebacker said. "Maybe I'll just wait until next year. I guess it wouldn't hurt to miss opening day just this once. I've never missed one. But it looks like I don't have much choice. What a shame . . ."

Dad glanced back at the car.

Noooooooooooo! That's what I wanted to scream.

"Well, I guess you could ride up there with us," Dad said.

"Excellent! You won't regret it," Mr. Humblebacker said. "I'm an experienced angler, and can teach the little lady all sorts of useful woods lore. This will be one opening day she'll never forget."

I know we're supposed to help other people, and share things, but this was a special day. I didn't want to share it.

When Dad got back to the car, he gave me a look that said, *I'm sorry, but what could I do?*

I responded with a look that said, *You could have thought of something.*

As I headed for the front seat, Mr. Humblebacker put his hand on my shoulder and said, "Do you mind if I ride up there? I get carsick in the back."

"Fine." It wasn't fine, but I knew there was no point making a fuss.

I napped a lot on the ride to Foley State Park. It wasn't easy. From the time we got in the car until the time we reached the small gravel parking lot by the trail that led to our favorite stretch of Foley's Creek, Mr. Humblebacker talked.

The air still had that morning crispness

when I got out of the car. The sun was up now. The stars were gone, though I could still see the tiniest hint of one bright one just above the tree line. It almost seemed as if it were following us, but I knew that was an illusion.

I loved the walk to the creek. One time, we came across a deer. Another time, we saw beavers in a small pond off to the side of the path. This year, I think Mr. Humblebacker scared all the wildlife away. Not only was he still yacking, but his stuff clanked a lot when he walked. It was like taking a stroll with a sack full of empty cans and marbles.

"We should move apart," I said when we reached the creek.

"Oh, what fun would that be?" Mr. Humblebacker said. "Fishing is all about companionship. And I'd hate for you to miss seeing all my great catches."

He dropped his tackle box at his feet with another rattling *clank*, leaned over, popped it open, and took out a huge lure. It looked like something you'd use in the ocean to fish for marlin or tuna. And it had treble hooks, which make it really hard to unhook the fish. Dad and I keep and eat what we catch, but we still wouldn't use that kind of hook.

"What in the world is that enormous thing?" Dad asked.

"You got to go big to catch big," Mr. Humblebacker said as he tied the lure to his line. "Tiny lures catch tiny trout."

Dad and I inched away from him and got our own lines ready. I didn't want to be anywhere near Mr. Humblebacker when he cast that monster.

I decided to use a spinner. I liked the way it flashed as I reeled it through the water. Just for fun, I picked the tiniest one I had. It was less than an inch long.

Even so, it was way bigger than what Dad was going to use. He loved to fly fish. That's kind of hard. You use tiny lures made of bits of feather and fur. They're tied together with thread so they look like the sort of insects trout enjoy slurping up. You had to whip the line back and forth, and set the fly down just right in the water so that it looked natural.

I checked my watch. Finally, it was eight o'clock. Time to fish. Opening day had started! I smiled at Dad. He smiled back. Maybe everything would be okay.

Just as I was about to make my first cast, a huge splash startled me. Mr. Humblebacker's lure had hit the water like a boulder dropped from an airplane.

"That's going to scare off all the fish," Dad said.

"He's not catching anything," I said. "And neither are we, probably. Not with all that noise."

"Got one!" Mr. Humblebacker screamed. "Wahooo!"

I couldn't believe it. He had a fish. From the splashing and the thrashing in the water, it had to be huge.

"No way . . ." I said to Dad. The wild trout in Foley's Creek didn't grow very big. There wasn't a fish in the whole creek that would have gone for that lure, or put up that hard a fight.

"Yeah. No way," Dad said, shaking his head.

Then, I saw why there was so much splashing.

"Snagged," Dad said as Mr. Humblebacker landed his catch.

"That's not legal," I said. "And it's really not fair."

Mr. Humblebacker hadn't caught the fish. He'd snagged its side with one of the treble hooks when he was cranking in the lure from the water.

"I'm going to tell him that's wrong." I decided it was my turn to shout. I started to stomp over there, but Dad stopped me.

"Let it go, Rachel," he said.

"But it's wrong," I said.

"I know." Dad put both hands on my shoulders and looked me right in the eye. "We can talk to him about it later. Nothing we say to him here will change things. He's too excited to listen to us. Right now, let's just try to enjoy our trip. Okay?"

"Okay." I sighed and looked up at the sky. The star was still there. It reminded me of the beautiful, perfect start to our trip, with a star-filled sky. People make a wish on the first star they see. Maybe I could make a wish on the last one. It was worth a try. *Fix things, last star,* I wished. *Please.*

And then, because I didn't have a lot of faith in wishes, and because Dad had asked, I did try to enjoy myself. I caught two trout with my itsy-bitsy spinner. Dad caught one with a fly. He didn't mind at all that I caught more. He loved fishing, and being out in nature with me. There was no need to keep score.

Though Mr. Humblebacker needed to. He counted out loud as he snagged five more fish, putting his total at six.

"One more and he's done," Dad whispered to me.

"If he follows the rules," I said. You were only allowed to catch seven fish each day.

That's when a really big fish came splashing downstream. It was so huge, its dorsal fin stuck out of the water, even in the deepest pools.

I stared. Dad stared. Mr. Humblebacker went right into action.

"Mine!" he shouted, casting his monster lure at the monster fish.

The instant the lure hit the water, the fish swallowed the whole thing. Then, it took off, zigzagging upstream. It pulled the line from Mr. Humblebacker's reel so fast, I was surprised the spool didn't catch fire.

Mr. Humblebacker managed to get the fish closer and closer as he battled against each run. Finally, he had it within reach. He let go of his rod with one hand and grabbed his landing net from his belt.

"What kind of fish is that?" I asked Dad.

"No idea," he said.

It didn't look like any trout I'd ever seen, or any other fish, though I knew there were some really bizarre creatures roaming the waters.

The top was shaped right. But I didn't see

any scales. The eyes seemed to be painted on. And there was no bottom half. It looked like someone had taken a fish and sawn off anything that went beneath the waterline.

"Don't touch it!" I screamed as I realized what it reminded me of.

Mr. Humblebacker flashed me a puzzled look, then reached out to scoop up the fish. As he did, it opened its mouth wider than I'd ever imagined was possible, swallowed the net, and kept going until Mr. Humblebacker's whole arm was engulfed. It no longer looked like a fish. It was now a glowing tube that shimmered and pulsed like it was made of energy.

I stared, too astonished to move. Dad dropped his rod and ran to help. But it was too late. The fish, and its catch, rose in the air like they were being reeled into the sky. I could see flickering bits of light above them, as if there

were an almost invisible line tied to the lure, or some sort of energy beam.

"Help!" Mr. Humblebacker screamed as he was reeled away.

Dad made one heroic leap, and almost managed to grab a foot. But he missed. And Mr. Humblebacker was pulled up toward a glowing light that was much closer and a lot brighter now. It was shaped more like a saucer than a star. I was pretty sure it wasn't Venus.

"He's gone," Dad said.

"Maybe he'll come back," I said. "Don't aliens just study people, erase their memories of the abduction, and then drop them off in the middle of a cornfield, or on a lonely country road?"

"You've been watching too many movies," Dad said. "We have no idea what they'll do."

"They won't eat him, will they?" I asked.

"I doubt it," Dad said. "If they're sophisticated enough to travel from another galaxy, I suspect that they have better sources of food."

"That's good," I said.

"Want to go home?" Dad asked.

I looked at the calm water, flowing past us as if nothing unusual had happened, and the sun rising well above the trees. "No. I want to fish," I said. And I wanted to enjoy daddy-daughter day the way it was meant to be—with just the two of us. We'd be getting a late start, but that was okay.

It was a good day, after all. Dad and I ended it together. We even stopped for milk shakes on the drive back home. And, as Mr. Humblebacker had promised, it was a day I'd never forget.

On the other hand, I think there were parts of the day he'd never remember. He showed up two days later, with no idea how he'd ended up stranded on top of the town's water tower, wearing nothing but his underwear and a hat.

He's still pretty loud and obnoxious, but

every once in a while, he'll stop talking right in the middle of a sentence, stare at the sky, and shudder. And he's never asked us to take him fishing again.

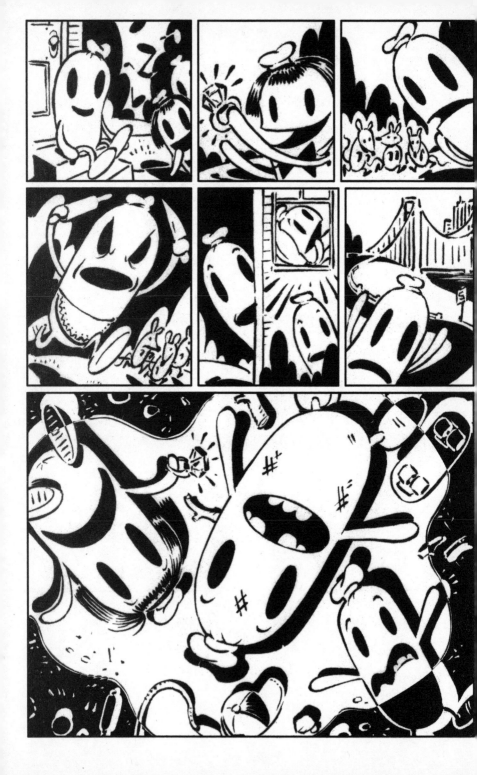

DANGER GOOSE

I was sitting on the front steps of my apartment building, completely bored. I must have been bored to start singing. I must have been really bored to start singing "Three Blind Mice." I caught myself after just a couple of lines. But I still felt like a total Weenie. And it was too late to keep from getting teased.

Mary and Chad, who were hanging out next door, started laughing and making fun of me. It was bad enough that I was singing, but it was worse that I was singing a kiddie song.

"How cute," Mary said. "Getting ready for the kindergarten talent show?"

"Mother Goose has come for a visit," Chad said. *"Honk! Honk!"* He laughed so hard at his own joke that he almost fell off the steps.

"Okay, give me a break," I said.

"Well, you made fun of me when I got this," Mary said. She held up the hand on which she'd put the ring she'd found in the box of cereal she was munching. She'd made a big deal out of it being a magic ring.

"Of course I did," I said. "There aren't any magic rings."

"Oh, yeah?" Mary said. "Well, I'll show you." She waved her hand at me and started spouting magic words like *abracadabra, hocus-pocus,* and *alakazam.*

Before I could tell her to stop being silly, something dashed down the street past us.

"Wow, those are mice," Chad said. He got up from the stoop and walked toward me.

"Three of them," Mary said as she joined us.

"Three blind mice," I said as I saw them stop at the curb, feel it with their paws, and sniff the air before crossing the street.

Chad pointed down the block. "I think they're chasing someone."

Sure enough, a woman was running ahead of the mice. She had a white scarf on her head, and an apron tied around her waist, like the people who worked in the fields in old paintings. "She's a farmer's wife," I said.

I thought about what I had sung:

Three blind mice,
Three blind mice,
See how they run,
See how they run,
They all ran after the farmer's wife.

I'd stopped singing before the part where she cuts off their tails with a carving knife. I guess that was a good thing for the mice.

After the mice and the farmer's wife ran out of sight, I looked at my friends. They looked at me. "Could it be . . . ?" I asked.

"Told you so," Mary said. "It's magic."

"I'll try another song," Chad said. He began to sing, *"Frère Jacques, Frère Jacques. Dormez vous? Dormez vous?"*

I thought that was a silly choice. All it meant was "Are you sleeping, brother John." But I didn't say anything.

Mary was less polite. "Come on," she yelled. "That's a stupid one to pick. Nothing's going to happen."

That was followed by a much louder shout.

"HEY, YOU KIDS! KEEP THE NOISE DOWN! I'M TRYING TO SLEEP!"

We looked up at a window in an apartment on the second floor of Chad's building. "Who's that?" Mary asked.

"You know Phil, the new kid who moved here last month?" Chad said.

"Sure," I said. "He's in band class with me."

"That's his older brother, John," Chad said. "He works nights. Guess we woke him."

We all looked at each other again. "So that song came to life, too," I said. "We have to find the right song to sing, next. We could make something amazing happen."

Mary started to sing, *"London Bridge is—"*

"Stop!" I shouted. I pointed down the street to the bridge that crossed over the river. "You want it to fall down?"

"It's not London Bridge," Mary said.

"But it's still a bridge. We shouldn't take any chances," I said. "No more singing until we discuss this. First, does it only work with nursery rhymes?"

"Who knows?" Chad said.

"Let's try something else," Mary said.

"I've got an idea." I ran inside and grabbed two bananas from the kitchen counter.

"What's that for?" Chad asked.

"I remembered an old song," I said. "It's

the perfect test." I put the bananas down and started singing a song my grandfather used to sing to me: "Yes! We Have No Bananas." It seemed like the perfect way to test the magic.

We all watched the bananas. They didn't vanish.

"We still have bananas," Mary said. She twisted the ring on her finger.

"And now I have that stupid song stuck in my head," Chad said.

"Must just be nursery rhymes." I took the bananas back to the kitchen, then joined my friends out front. We tried to think of a good song to sing. Most of the titles we came up with didn't seem like they would do anything good. We didn't want to produce a farmer in a dell or see a cow jump over the moon. I'm pretty sure that would be bad for the cow. And Mary was very clear that she did not want a little lamb—especially not one that would follow her to school.

"There has to be a great one we aren't thinking of," Chad said.

"Let's make a list of nursery rhymes," I said.

"Nursery rhymes!" someone said.

I turned around, and saw my friend Bobby. "Help us think up nursery rhymes," I said.

"Sure." He smiled, and then, instead of listing them, he started to sing one. It seemed harmless, so I didn't stop him.

"Ring around the rosy, pocket full of posies . . ."

As he sang those words, I felt something fill up my pocket. I didn't have to look. I knew what it was. Bobby kept singing: *"Ashes, ashes, we all fall down!"*

Too late, I remembered about that line. And, yeah, as ashes filled the air and tickled our noses, we sneezed so violently we all fell down. Bobby smacked his shoulder pretty hard. Chad lost a tooth. It was loose, anyhow, so it wasn't a big deal. I broke my nose. I've done that twice before, thanks to my skateboard. So I guess that wasn't a big deal, either.

But Mary broke the magic ring, which I guess was a big deal. But I also guess it wasn't a bad thing. There were probably plenty of other dangerous songs out there. Who knew kiddie songs could be so painful?

A NEW WRINKLE

I was playing over at my friend Dan's house when I spotted the plastic squeeze bottle in the trash.

"What's this?" I asked.

"Mom uses it," Dan said. "I guess she threw it out because it expired or something." His mom is a dermatologist. She helps people with skin problems.

I read the label: *WrinkleOut*. Then I tried to pronounce the name of the main ingredient: "OnabotulismtoxinA. What's that do?"

"I think it freezes the muscles or something," Dan said. "All I know is that people come into her office with a lot of wrinkles, and leave with a smooth face. And a smile. It makes them happy."

Dan took the bottle from me and squirted an ant that was crawling along the sidewalk. It stopped in its tracks. "No more wrinkles for you," he said.

Just then, a fly buzzed right past my face. I grabbed the bottle from Dan and sprayed the fly.

It froze.

I don't mean it stopped flying and fell to the ground. I mean, it froze right where it was, like someone had hit a PAUSE button.

"Wow . . ." I tapped the fly. It slid through the air, but stayed frozen.

Dan and I both looked around. I guess he had the same idea I did—what else could we freeze?

He grabbed the bottle and ran around to his backyard, freezing a butterfly and a couple beetles along the way.

I grabbed the bottle and froze another

ant. That's when we saw the squirrel. It was leaping from branch to branch on an apple tree, near the trash where I'd found the bottle. I figured it would be awesome to freeze the squirrel in midair.

"My turn," Dan said, grabbing for the bottle.

"No, it isn't." I jerked my hand away.

"Share," Dan said. "My mom threw it out."

"I found it." I dashed off, cutting toward the apple tree.

Dan caught up, and made a grab for my shoulder. I pulled free, and managed to smack my head on a low branch.

"Ow!" I felt a bad scratch under my eye.

"That's going to sting a little," Dan said. He started laughing.

Before I could say anything, something fell from the tree and bonked him on the head. It wasn't an apple. It was big and gray.

"Hah!" I said as Dan flinched and grabbed

his head. "You deserved that." His pain made me happy.

And then, a thought wiped my smile away.

Apples aren't big and gray.

And they usually don't fall off trees in the early summer. I had a terrible feeling I knew what had smacked Dan. When I looked down, and saw I was right, my whole body got hit by a jolt of fear.

"Wasps!" I shouted.

I'd knocked a nest loose when I slammed into the tree.

A buzz filled the air as angry wasps streamed out of the broken nest.

My brain screamed *RUN!* But I guess it also sent a message to my hands. Acting without even thinking, I sprayed the wasps, and drenched the nest.

The wasps, both in the air and in the nest, all froze.

"Good thinking," Dan said. "You saved us. You really are a genius. I'm amazed at your reflexes. You are such a quick thinker. Brilliant.

Totally brilliant. Smartest kid on the block.
Maybe even in the whole world."

Just as I realized he was trying to
distract me with compliments, he
shot his hand out and snatched the
bottle from me.

"Sucker," he said.

I grabbed his arm as he tried to
turn away. We wrestled. I lost my balance, but
pulled him down with me as we fell.

I guess he squeezed the bottle by accident, because I felt a wet spray wash over my
face. My body jolted to a stop before it hit
the ground. I was frozen. So was Dan. I could
barely see him, and I couldn't move my eyes.
But I could see right in front of my face. And
I did not like what I saw at all.

I'd been about to fall right on the wasp nest.

My nose was inches from it. Frozen
wasps were all around me. I couldn't
feel my face, but I was pretty sure
there were wasps pressing right
against it. It's a good thing they
couldn't move.

I hoped we wouldn't be frozen forever. My lips wouldn't move, but I could sort of move my tongue. I tried to say, *This'll wear off, right?* It came out, "Issl ear oth, ight?"

"I oat so," Dan said. *I hope so.*

I didn't bother trying to say anything else. After a while, I found I could move my eyes a bit. That's when I spotted the ant that Dan had frozen. Just as I looked at it, it started to crawl. I looked at the fly I'd sprayed. It was still frozen. But not for long. In a moment, it flew off.

I thought about what I'd just seen. First the ant had unfrozen, and then the fly.

That meant . . .

"Oh no!" I gasped, almost speaking clearly.

"Ut?" Dan asked.

"Wasps next," I said.

Everything was unfreezing in the order it had been frozen. First the ant, then the fly. After that, the butterfly and the beetles. The wasps would be next, and I was pretty sure they would still be angry.

And when they unfroze, there was no way we could run from them, because we'd still be frozen.

Worse, when we unfroze, we'd finish our fall, and land right on top of the nest.

The wasps started to move.

One landed on my nose.

I felt myself falling.

This was going to sting.

A lot.

ABOUT THE AUTHOR

DAVID LUBAR credits his passion for short stories to his limited attention span and bad typing skills, though he has been known to sit still and peck at the keyboard long enough to write a novel or chapter book now and then, including *Hidden Talents* (an ALA Best Book for Young Adults) and *My Rotten Life,* which is currently under development for a cartoon series. He lives in Nazareth, Pennsylvania, with his amazing wife, and not too far from his amazing daughter. In his spare time, he takes naps on the couch.

ABOUT THE ILLUSTRATOR

BILL MAYER is absolutely amazing. Bill's crazy creatures, characters, and comic creations have been sought after for magazine covers, countless articles, and even stamps for the U.S. Postal Service. He has won almost every illustration award known to man and even some known to fish. Bill and his wife live in Decatur, Georgia. They have a son and three grandsons.